This book belongs to...

In loving memory of Aunt Mig. —C.C.

Other Dr. Hippo Stories

The Little Elephant with the Big Earache

Peeper Has a Fever

Katie Caught a Cold

Upcoming books from The Hippocratic Press

Look for Dr. Hippo in upcoming stories: *The Moose with Loose Poops* is coming soon!

Ordering information

Order books from your local book retailer, your online book source, or directly from:

The Hippocratic Press

281A Fairhaven Hill Road

Concord, MA 01742

www.hippocraticpress.com

Text and illustrations copyright © The Hippocratic Press, LLC. 2006. All rights reserved.

First American edition 2006 published by The Hippocratic Press.

Charlotte Cowan, M.D. and Katy Bratun assert the right to be identified as the author and the illustrator of this work.

Printed in China.

Library of Congress Control Number: 2006923072

ISBN 0-9753516-4-8

Sadie's Sore Throat

by Charlotte Cowan, M.D.   *illustrated by* Katy Bratun

book design by Labor Day Creative

THE HIPPOCRATIC PRESS
CONCORD, MA

Sadie looked up. "Mom," she asked, "Will they like my necklaces?"

"Of course," her mother answered. "They're perfect for the Fair! Maybe you'll even win a prize!"

"But what can I make?" asked Barley.

"We'll get rocks from the river," said their Mom, "to make into paperweights."

"Look for smooth rocks in different shapes, Barley."

He picked up a long, skinny stone. "This'll be a good snake," he laughed. "Let's go show Sadie."

"Sadie," asked her Mom, "is something wrong? You've hardly touched your snack."

"I'm not hungry," she answered, "and the juice doesn't taste good."

"But you love orange juice!"

"It hurts to swallow, Mom. And I have a tummy ache, too."

"Buttercup, you're as hot as the sun! Let's go take your temperature."

"102°!" she exclaimed a minute later. "You're *sick*, sweetheart! I bet something's wrong with your throat."

Sadie frowned. "But I have to be well for the Fair, Mom!"

"We'll see. I'll call Dr. Hippo after you take this medicine. It'll help you feel better and lower your fever, too."

"But it hurts to *swallow!*"

"I know. A popsicle might taste good though. What's your favorite flavor?"

"Purple polka dot," said Sadie.

Sadie walked slowly. "I don't have to see Dr. Hippo," she said. "That medicine made me *all* better."

"I know you feel better, Sadie, but Dr. Hippo still needs to tell us what's wrong," said her Mom.

"No," said Sadie. "I'm *not* going."

"We *need* to go," insisted her mother, "but we'll visit Grandma and Barley later."

"Please read me this book," begged Sadie. "It's about an elephant."

"*The Little Elephant with the Big Earache*," began her Mom.

Sadie listened. "Poor little elephant," she said. "He's sick, too!"

Dr. Hippo appeared. "Hello, Sadie," he said. "Imagine getting sick before the Fair! Come on in!"

Sadie smiled.

"I'm *six* now and I'm making necklaces to sell," she said.

"You've had a birthday!" said Dr. Hippo. "How wonderful!"

"Sadie has a fever and a *terrible* sore throat," explained her Mom.

"And my tummy hurts, too," added Sadie.

"Gracious!" said Dr. Hippo. "Let's try to get you better."

"Sadie, I'd like to listen to your heart and lungs and then look into your ears and mouth." Dr. Hippo paused. "That will help me find out what's wrong. Does that make sense?"

Sadie nodded. "But don't hurt Monkey," she said.

"I'll be careful of you both," promised Dr. Hippo.

"You have a good heart, Sadie."

"Pretend to blow up a big balloon!"

"No butterflies in your ears today!"

"Sadie, so far you and Monkey both look fine," smiled Dr. Hippo. "Please open your mouth and stick your tongue *way* out."

"Hmm," he noted, "your throat looks red this morning. Maybe you have a strep throat: that would make it *very* sore."

"I know," she said. "It *hurts!*"

Dr. Hippo continued: "To test for strep, I need to touch this cotton swab to the back of your throat. It won't hurt, but it might feel funny for a second. I'll be done before you can say, 'Spunky Monkey!'"

Dr. Hippo showed Sadie a big
box. "Pick a sticker," he said.
"And take one for Monkey, too:
You both did a great job!"

"Thank you," she said,
choosing two stickers.

"Sadie's throat swab showed strep—a bacterial infection—and so I've prescribed an antibiotic for her," said Dr. Hippo. "She should feel *much* better soon, especially if you give her pain medicine and popsicles. But please keep in touch with me."

"Thanks, Dr. Hippo," said Sadie's Mom. "I'll call if I get worried."

"Don't forget about ice cream and popsicles," said Dr. Hippo. "They're *great* for sore throats!"

"And for little Monkeys, too," smiled Sadie.

"I'm sick," announced Sadie.

"We thought you might be," said Grandma. "We made you something to help you feel better."

"I made you a *caterpillar!*" said Barley. "Come see!"

"Thanks, Barley," laughed Sadie.

"We made you ice pops, too," offered Barley.

"Yum!" said Sadie, reaching for a star.

"Sweet Buttercup, you and I should
go home for a nap," said her Mom,
"but Barley can stay here."

"Okay," yawned Sadie.
"I'm tired anyway."

"Take care, little one,"
said Grandma.

"Mom," said Sadie, "I have a surprise for the Fair."

"What is it?" asked her Mom. "Can we make it together?"

"No thanks, Mom," smiled Sadie. "It's a secret."

"You'll feel better soon, sweetheart. We can make cookies tomorrow while you're home from school."

"Okay," said Sadie, "I'll be busy with my beads, too."

Many popsicles and a few days later,
Sadie felt like new.

"I'm so excited about the Fair!" she said.

"Me, too!" added Barley.

"Me three," laughed Grandma.

"Where's my Sadie?" asked her mother.
"It's almost time for the judges!"

"They're coming this way!"
observed Grandma.

JUNGLE JEWELS

ROCKS THAT ROCK

"Sweet Buttercup," exclaimed
her Mom, "you're just in time!"

The little giraffe laughed:
"Surprise!" she said.

Dr. Hippo chuckled:
"Sadie's all well—with
a *necklace* to sell!"

He smiled. "Glad you're
feeling better, six year old!"

The Fair was almost over when the Principal spoke:

"Thank you for coming, boys and girls, and for working so hard for our Fair! Now let's give out the prizes. In first place..."

He smiled: "An award winning necklace by a young *lady*...

Come up for your prize, *popsicle Sadie!*"